This book is dedicated to the community teachers who taught me poetry
and the power of song. To my first teacher in creativity and the joys of
being different and unique, my grandmother Verdia Belle Coleman Ross:
Your songs and love carry me through some of my roughest hours.
To my mom Donna Williams, who filled my world with poetry and
poets I never heard about in school: Thanks for making me learn
a couple of songs and encouraging me to sing.

I like to sing.

Sometimes my big sister says my voice is annoying and that I need to stop singing.

But my mama tells me to feel free to sing and be fully me, to feel free to sing my melody.

She says I'm free to share my songs and bare my heart, to not worry about others, I should just start.

If you're happy and
you know it...

I can Sing
when I'm happy.

I can sing the alphabet song
to my baby brother.

I can sing to the rain.

I can sing lullabies to help my brother go to sleep.

Fannie Lou Hamer
sang in the fight
for voting rights.
She asked others to
shine their lights.

I don't have
to sound perfect
to make a difference.
I can use my voice
like the Freedom Fighters
who sang in resistance.

The Freedom Fighters
Sang on buses
and in the streets,

taking risks
and sitting in
lunch counter
seats.

They sang songs like
"Oh Freedom" and
"We Shall Overcome."

They sang songs that brought hope to everyone.

I can sing
when I'm feeling down.

I can sing to
turn things around.

I can sing to make
others feel better.
I can sing and
dance like
Josephine Baker.

There are lots of reasons why people sing. They sing to help people feel better, to tell a story, or just to share how they're feeling.

Sheryl Davis is a passionate advocate for equity, and educational opportunity. Davis is the creator of the *Everybody Reads*—a summer learning, family literacy, and reading development initiative centering BIPOC youth. Throughout her career and many roles, she has continued to design programs and curriculum centered around social justice, racial equity, student wellness and achievement.